P9-CKS-137

This book is a gift of the
Friends of the Orinda Library

Join us at
friendsoftheorindalibrary.org

SandCastle™

Signs of the Seasons

SIGNS OF
Summer

Colleen Dolphin

Consulting Editor,
Diane Craig, M.A./Reading Specialist

A Division of ABDO

ABDO
Publishing Company

visit us at www.abdopublishing.com

Published by ABDO Publishing Company, a division of ABDO, P.O. Box 398166, Minneapolis, Minnesota 55439. Copyright © 2013 by Abdo Consulting Group, Inc. International copyrights reserved in all countries. No part of this book may be reproduced in any form without written permission from the publisher. SandCastle™ is a trademark and logo of ABDO Publishing Company.

Printed in the United States of America, North Mankato, Minnesota
062012
092012

 PRINTED ON RECYCLED PAPER

Editor: Liz Salzmann
Content Developer: Nancy Tuminelly
Cover and Interior Design and Production: Colleen Dolphin, Mighty Media, Inc.
Photo Credits: Holly Bergstrom, Shutterstock

Library of Congress Cataloging-in-Publication Data
Dolphin, Colleen, 1979-
  Signs of summer / Colleen Dolphin.
     p. cm. -- (Signs of the seasons)
  ISBN 978-1-61783-394-6
  1. Summer--Juvenile literature. 2. Seasons--Juvenile literature. I. Title.
  QB637.6.D65 2013
  508.2--dc23
                        2011052131

SandCastle™ Level: Beginning

SandCastle™ books are created by a team of professional educators, reading specialists, and content developers around five essential components—phonemic awareness, phonics, vocabulary, text comprehension, and fluency—to assist young readers as they develop reading skills and strategies and increase their general knowledge. All books are written, reviewed, and leveled for guided reading, early reading intervention, and Accelerated Reader® programs for use in shared, guided, and independent reading and writing activities to support a balanced approach to literacy instruction. The SandCastle™ series has four levels that correspond to early literacy development. The levels are provided to help teachers and parents select appropriate books for young readers.

Emerging Readers (no flags)

Beginning Readers (1 flag)

Transitional Readers (2 flags)

Fluent Readers (3 flags)

contents

seasons

There are four seasons during the year. They are called spring, summer, autumn, and winter. The weather, plants, animals, and daylight hours **change** during each season.

summer

spring

winter

autumn

summer

During the year, Earth travels around the sun. This brings some parts of Earth closer to the sun. Other parts of Earth get farther from the sun. Summer happens in the parts closest to the sun.

DID YOU KNOW?
In Canada it is summer in July. In Australia it is summer in December.

8

It is warm in the summer.
The sky can be very blue.
The clouds can be white and
fluffy when the sun is out.

There is a lot of daylight in summer. It does not get dark out until late in the evening. Dave likes to help build a fire when he goes camping. He starts before it gets dark outside.

There are many plants and flowers that grow in the summer. Ty, Jenny, Mike, and Laura like to **hike** in the woods. They look at all the plants around them.

It is fun to garden in the summer. The warm **temperature** helps **fruits** and **vegetables** grow. Brooklyn loves to eat them **fresh** from the garden!

Animals like to run and play in the summer. There are plenty of plants and grass for them to eat.

DID YOU KNOW?
Summer comes after spring and before autumn.

17

Ally and Jamie like to play in the pool when it's hot outside. Swimming keeps them cool in the summer.

Henry and his brother like to fish in the summer. What do you like to do? Do you play outside in the nice, warm weather?

summer activities

PLAY HIDE AND SEEK!

GO SNORKELING!

RUN THROUGH A SPRINKLER!

PLAY SUMMER SPORTS.

summer quiz

Read each sentence below. Then decide if it is true or false.

1. It is cold during the summer.
   True or False?

2. There is a lot of daylight in summer.
   True or False?

3. Plants and flowers grow in the summer.
   True or False?

4. Summer is not a good time for gardening.
   True or False?

5. Animals like to play in the summer.
   True or False?

glossary

change – to be altered or become different.

fluffy – light, soft, and airy.

fresh – just picked from the garden.

fruit – the fleshy, sweet part of a tree or plant that contains one or more seeds.

hike – to take a long walk, especially in the country.

temperature – a measure of how hot or cold something is.

vegetable – the edible part of a plant grown for food.